Dedicated to Kenneth G. Sivulich, my husband and friend, thank you for taking me on such a challenging journey!

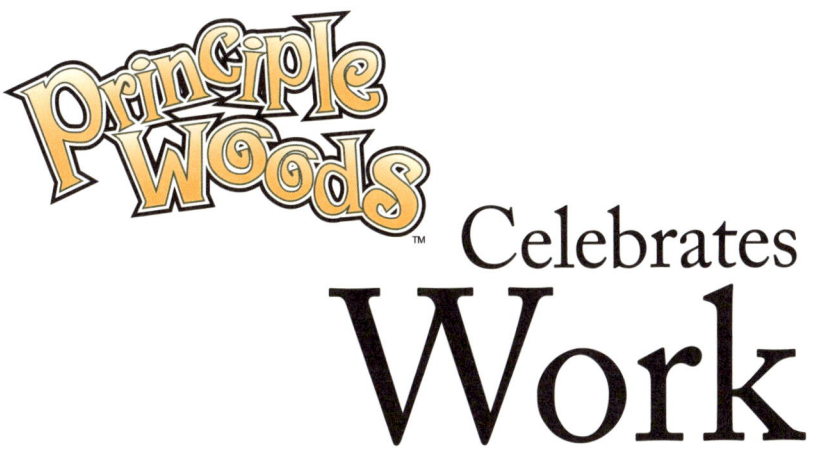# Celebrates Work

Author
Sandra Stroner Sivulich

Illustrator
Kevin Shore

 Principle Woods, Inc.
One San Jose Place, Suite 11
Jacksonville, Florida 32257
www.principlewoods.com

This book is a work of fiction. Names, characters, places, and incidents either are products of the author's imagination or are used fictitiously. Any resemblance to actual events or locales or persons, living or dead, is entirely coincidental.

Text copyright © 2003 by Principle Woods, Inc.
Illustrations copyright © 2003 by Principle Woods, Inc.
All rights reserved. No part of this book may be used or reproduced in any manner without the prior written permission of Principle Woods, Inc.

Designed by David Whitlock, Principle Design Group, Inc.

Printed in Singapore

0203-01ED
ISBN 0-9719228-2-9

Contents

Story One
Less Mess 6

Story Two
The Shoulds and the Coulds 24

Story Three
The Garden Team 44

Less Mess

Tipper's treehouse was a mess. Nothing was put away where it belonged. Things were piled on top of each other. Because nothing was in its place, Tipper could not find what he needed. What he needed was his red hat—his "lucky" red hat. Springer and he were going to play a very important game, and he needed to wear his lucky hat. No matter how hard he looked, however, he could not find the hat. His house became more messy the more he looked. And the more he looked, the madder he got. He was not mad at his house. He was not mad at his hat. He was just mad at EVERYTHING.

He started to walk around Great Pine in circles because there was no place to sit down.

Finally, he just sat in the middle of the floor and shouted out, "I do not like what is happening to me! I am not happy. I am not happy because everything is a mess. I am not happy because I cannot find anything. I must fix what is happening. I must start to put things back in their place so I can find what I need, when I need it."

Tipper looked around. Where would he begin? How would he do this big job? There was too much to do. It would be easier to put the job off. It would be easier to walk away. And so he did. He left his treehouse without his lucky hat and walked to the meadow.

"Hey, Tipper," said Springer. "Are you ready to play? Are you ready to win?"

"Yeah, I guess so," said Tipper in a quiet voice.

"Is anything wrong, Tipper?" asked Springer. "You do not seem to be happy about playing. Where is your lucky hat?"

"I could not find it," answered Tipper sadly. "I cannot find anything. I do not know what to do. The job of putting my house in order is too big. I don't know how it got so messy in the first place. And I do not know how to even begin to fix it."

"Maybe we need to ask Sage to help you. She knows how to fix things. Sometimes we have to ask others for help when we do not know what to do," Springer gently told his friend.

So, instead of playing their game, Springer and Tipper went to find Sage.

Tipper almost ran over Sage, he was in such a hurry to find her. "Help me, Sage," he begged. "Can you help me have less mess? Can you help me find my hat? Can you help me?"

When Sage heard the problem, she nodded her head in an understanding way. "Yes, Tipper, I know. Sometimes a job may look too big for us to do. Sometimes we do not even know where to start. Sometimes a job is so big, we can only see the end and do not know how to get there.

"It would be nice if we had a map we could follow to the end. I am going to tell you a little secret on how to get your work done even when the job seems too big.

"Here is all you have to do: 1. Start! 2. Break up the job into small chunks or parts. Do one small job at a time. For example, put away only one pile of junk—not everything at once. Stop and tell yourself, 'Good job. I finished what I wanted to do.' 3. Give yourself

a little treat to celebrate the fact that you finished the job. 4. Go on to the next little job and do the same thing. Finish it and stop. You have another success.

"Little by little, success after success, you will finish the whole, big job. In fact, probably you will surprise yourself when you are done because it happened faster than you thought it would.

"Remember, your house got messy little by little. So you have to clean it up the same way—little by little."

"Well…I guess that makes sense," said Tipper slowly, "but it's not exactly what I wanted to hear. I wanted you to tell me how I could make my mess less WITHOUT any work."

"Tipper, dear Tipper," Sage said, smiling to herself, "I know you would rather play than work. So why don't you make a little game out of your work?"

"Thank you, Sage, that is a great idea! I know just what I'll do," said Tipper in an excited voice. "I will call my game, 'Little By Little.' Each time I finish a little job, I'll give myself a point. I'm sure I will win. In fact, I'll be the champion of Principle Woods!

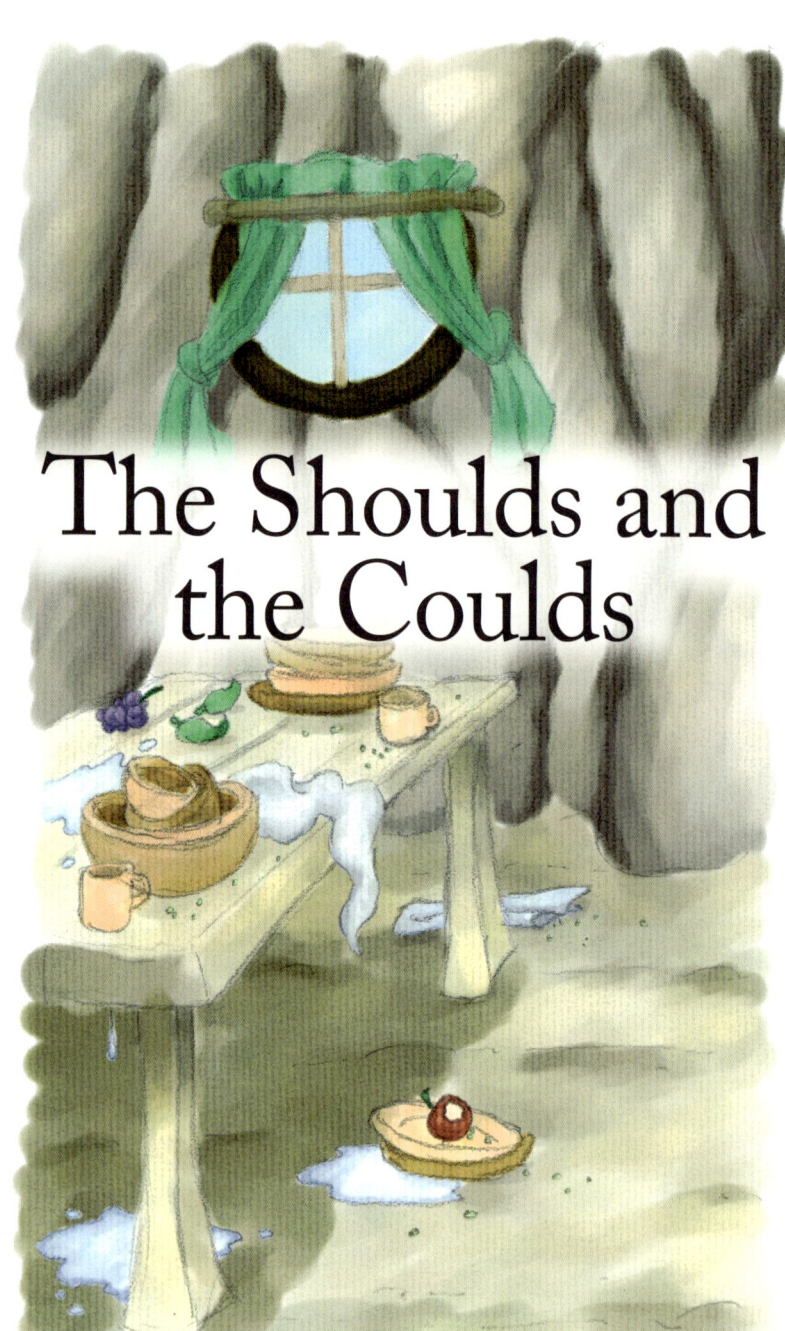

The Shoulds and the Coulds

"I should be cleaning my clubhouse," thought Blossom, the skunk, "but I think I'll try on my new hats one more time. I look so pretty in all of them."

After Blossom tried on her fancy hats again and again, she decided it wasn't as much fun as it once was. She looked around the clubhouse. "I know I should clean. I know I could clean, but I don't want to. Maybe, I'll just pretend I'm cleaning. Instead of sweeping the floor, I'll hide the dirt under the rug. Instead of washing the windows, I'll close the curtains. Instead of putting things away, I'll pile them under a blanket. Who will know but me?"

Down at Busy Beaver Creek, Grinder, the beaver, was having the same problem. "I should be chopping more wood for the dam," he thought, "but I think I'll play a little while longer."

After Grinder splashed and swam in Busy Beaver Creek, he got tired. It wasn't fun anymore. He looked at the tiny pile of wood that had been chopped for the dam. He could chop more. He knew he should chop more. "Maybe" he said, "I'll just pretend I'm chopping. Instead of getting a big tree and chopping it up, I'll make it look like I have a big pile by piling leaves and sticks underneath and covering the top with the big pieces. Who will know but me?"

Down by Great Pine, Tipper was having the same problem. "I should be gathering nuts and berries," he thought, "but I could just sit here under my tree and think about new games Springer and I can play."

After Tipper sat and thought about new games, he got bored. It wasn't fun anymore. He thought about his small pile of nuts and berries. "I know I should gather more. I know I could gather more, but I don't want to. Maybe, I'll just pretend I'm gathering. I'll do just a little. I'll put up a sign, 'Come and Play the Nut and Berry Game'. I'll tell all my friends whoever brings the most nuts and berries wins the game. They all like to win and so they will be happy. I will keep the nuts and berries and so I will be happy, too."

The next day, Blossom looked around her clubhouse. She did not like what she saw. So she left and went for a walk.

Grinder looked at his pile of wood. He did not like what he saw. So, he left and went for a walk.

Tipper looked at his empty table. He did not like what he saw. So, he left and went for a walk.

"Well, well, well, and how do you do?" asked Blossom as she saw her two friends coming along the path. "I thought you'd both be working. How come you're taking a walk?"

Tipper answered, "Well, the same goes for you, Blossom. You're supposed to be working, not walking. What's going on?"

Blossom looked at Grinder and Tipper and sadly said, "I don't know. All I know is something is not right. Playing all the time didn't make me happy because I knew I should be working. So, I decided instead of working a lot, I'd just work a little. But...I still don't feel happy. Getting only half the job done is not fun either."

Tipper and Grinder nodded their heads in agreement. "We know what you mean," they said together.

Just then, they saw Burly, the bear, coming along the path from a day of fishing. "Hello there, my fine friends. I hope you all are as good as I am. I had a wonderful day of work catching fish." As he got closer, he saw their sad faces.

"Well, I'm glad somebody had a good day," said Tipper gloomily. "When we play, we're not happy. But when we work halfway, we're not happy either. What are we going to do?"

"Well, I may not know the answers to a lot of questions, but I sure do know this answer," Burly proudly said. "You shouldn't work all the time, and you shouldn't play all the time either. You wouldn't play half a game, and so you can't do just half a job either. Do your work ALL the way until it's finished.

Today the best work you can do. Come back tomorrow and tell me if you think I gave you the right answer."

Blossom, Grinder, and Tipper all went back to their homes. They did their work the way they should; the way they knew they could. Blossom looked around the clubhouse and was happy. Doing the job the right way had not taken as long as she thought, and now she had time to try on more hats in a clean clubhouse.

Grinder looked at his big, real pile of chopped wood and was happy. It, too, had not taken too long, and he had time for a swim in Busy Beaver Creek.

Tipper gathered a huge pile of nuts and berries. He went running around Principle Woods shouting, "I'm the winner of my new game because I got the most nuts and berries! I'm the winner!"

The next day, Blossom, Grinder, and Tipper met Burly and told him he was right. Burly smiled a big Burly Bear smile and said, "Even though you didn't all play Tipper's game, you are all winners of another game. I call it the 'Why-Not-Do-It-Right Game'. Work should and could be as much fun as play if we just get going and do it the right way in the first place!"

The Garden Team

"Grinder, hurry up, hurry up! I need you to finish digging those two rows right now!" shouted Chopsie, the bossy beaver.

Everyone could hear Chopsie giving orders. Tipper, the squirrel, came up to Grinder, the beaver, and said in a mocking voice, "Grinder, hurry up, hurry up! I need you to finish digging those two rows right now!"

"Oh, hi, Tipper," said Grinder, when he saw his friend. "Do you need me to dig some rows for you, too?"

"No, my overworked friend, I do not. I was just making fun of your favorite boss, Miss Chopsie," answered Tipper. "Tell me, please, what all the fuss is about. She's shouting orders just like a general."

"Oh, Tipper, I'm surprised you haven't heard what's going on," said Grinder. "We are all working on a Principle Woods garden. Everyone heard the invitation to work. Why didn't you?"

"Oh, so that's what that invitation was," said Tipper. "I didn't pay too much attention to it. When I heard the word 'work' I covered my ears and didn't listen to the rest. I don't want to have anything to do with work. It's more fun to just play and do whatever you feel like."

"Oh, no, Tipper," answered Grinder, "You better not let Chopsie hear you say that. You will really be in trouble. Chopsie loves to work and she says everybody else should, too."

"Ha!" laughed Tipper. "That's the silliest thing I ever heard. Let her speak for herself. Besides, I do work hard. I work hard at getting out of work!" Tipper laughed again as he skipped over to see what everyone was doing.

"Hi, my busy, busy friends. What is everyone doing?" asked Tipper.

"Well," answered Burly, the bear, "It's about time you showed up! As the invitation said, we are making a Principle Woods Community Garden.

Each animal gets a row in the garden. Each animal plants what he likes to eat. Each animal has a certain job he does to make the garden grow."

"Yes," Grinder said in an excited voice. "Since Chopsie and I are the very best diggers in Principle Woods, we have to dig the garden and get the soil ready so the seeds can be planted."

"Of course, no one would know where anything was planted if there was not a sign on each row to tell them what was growing. Not only am I in charge of the signs, but I am also making a map of the whole garden," explained Blossom. "My job is the most important of all."

"Now, wait a minute, Blossom," interrupted Burly. "I think you may not be right this time. My job is very important, too. It is my job to bring water to the garden. Without water, we would have no garden at all. So my job is, indeed, quite important," stated Burly.

"Now, just wait, Burly!" shouted Springer. "What about my job? Because I am such a good hopper, I hop from row to row planting the seeds. If it wasn't for me, nothing would grow in the garden. It is very easy to see that my job is the most important.  So there!" said Springer as he hopped about in a circle.

At that point, all the animals started to shout. They were all trying to tell Tipper that their job was the most

important. For the first time in his life, Tipper was not the one making the noise. He was trying hard to listen, but it was so noisy, he was having a hard time.

The noise reached Sage, the owl, as she flew overhead. "Settle down, settle

down," she told her friends as she circled lower and lower. When she got low enough for them to see and hear her, they all quieted down. "Now," said Sage, as she landed on a low branch, "I need all of you to listen to me.

Everyone has an important job. Each job is as important as the other. In fact, each job needs the other. You are a team. You must work together."

Finally Tipper spoke up, "Oh, I get it. If we put the words "team" and "work" together, we have a new word— 'teamwork'. Without all of you, there would be no garden."

"Very good, Tipper," said Sage with a smile in her voice. "I am so proud of you because you understand that everyone is EQUALLY important."

"Well, I guess that makes me the smartest one here!" Tipper stated.

"Oh, no, it doesn't," interrupted Blossom. "You aren't so smart after all. You see, we all have a  row in the garden. When the garden blooms, we will all have good things to eat. Everyone except you, because you didn't work at all. Just knowing and talking about something doesn't get you on the team. You have to do something about it, too. So there, Mr. Smarty Pants Tipper!"

"My name is not Mr. Smarty Pants Tipper!" shouted Tipper.

When he shouted at Blossom, all the other animals started shouting, too. They shouted about the garden. They shouted about teamwork. They shouted about who was smart. They shouted about who was important.

Sage slowly circled the crowd and then flew high into the sky, shaking her head and grinning, "Well, they might not yet be a team, but at least they are together!"

Burly stepped into the group and said, "Everyone, please be quiet, I have something important to say. Tipper, why don't you really get smart and plant your row so you can join the team right now?"

Everyone looked at Tipper. Tipper looked back at all his friends. He thought about what Burly had said, and then with a big smile on his face, he said, "What a good idea! I'm surprised I didn't think of that myself. Just show me where I start to work."

All the animals cheered as they welcomed the newest member of the Garden Team.